This book belongs to

_____

MICKEY
MEETS THE GIANT

VOLUME 1

WALT DISNEY FUN-TO-READ LIBRARY

A BANTAM BOOK
TORONTO • NEW YORK • LONDON • SYDNEY • AUCKLAND

Mickey Meets the Giant   A Bantam Book/January 1986   All rights reserved.   Copyright © 1986 Walt Disney
Productions.   This book may not be reproduced, in whole or in part, by mimeograph or any other means.

ISBN 0-553-05573-9

Published simultaneously in the United States and Canada.   Bantam Books are published by Bantam Books, Inc.   Its
trademark, consisting of the words "Bantam Books" and the portrayal of a rooster, is Registered in U.S. Patent and
Trademark Office and in other countries.   Marca Registrada.   Bantam Books, Inc., 666 Fifth Avenue, New York,
New York 10103.   Printed in the United States of America   0 9 8 7 6 5 4 3 2 1

Once upon a time, there lived a brave woodcutter named Mickey. His work took him from place to place.

One day he came to a pretty town. It was called Cedar Grove.

"These hills are just full of sweet-smelling trees," he thought. "I can sell that wood. I'll make a lot of money. But first I must be sure my ax is sharp."

So the woodcutter walked through the streets of the town. There were many people in the street. Everyone looked very upset.

"Whatever will happen to us?" one woman cried.

"We must find someone who can beat
the giant," yelled a man.
"Why is everyone so afraid of this giant?
What has he done?" asked Mickey.

The people told him about a night when the giant decided to have a little fun. While they lay sleeping, the giant began to whistle. When he whistled, the wind blew.

He whistled through their windows. The wind blew through their homes. It blew all the sleeping people right out of their beds!

Mickey didn't like that story very much. And he didn't like the next one at all.

One day, the giant wanted to play. He jumped rope in the fields. They had just been planted. He made footprints all over the fields.

That night, it rained. The next day, the
fields were covered with foot-shaped lakes.

When the giant saw his footprints filled with water, he began to laugh. He laughed so hard that he fell down. He rolled on the ground. He laughed some more. Everything for miles around shook as he laughed.

This was too much for the animals in the forest. They were so afraid that they ran for their lives.

"Now there are no animals in Cedar Grove," said the giant. "And soon there will be no people! Ho, ho!"

"What a terrible giant!" thought Mickey.
Just then a wagon came racing into town. It
stopped. The driver jumped to the ground. He
told Mickey his story.

"I was taking my family away from Cedar Grove. But a huge boulder rolled right onto the road. It was so big! There was no way around it. I looked up to see where it came from. There stood the giant!

"The giant laughed very hard when he
saw that I was afraid. His laugh was as loud
as thunder. My horse was so scared that he
turned right around. He ran as fast as he
could—back here to Cedar Grove."

The giant had blocked the only way out
of town. Now the people of Cedar Grove
were trapped!

The brave woodcutter had heard enough.
"Let me face the giant," he said. "I have
beaten bullies before. I'll do it again!"
Everyone laughed at the woodcutter.

"You could not beat this giant," said a
kind policeman. "But I do think you must be
a very brave young man.

"Stan Dolittle is the man to do this," said the policeman. "I remember the time that Stan ran a mean old bear out of Cedar Grove."

Stan stepped to the front. "I will show the giant who is boss," he said.

But it was not long before Stan came running home. He was dripping wet, and he was very upset.

The giant had picked up poor Stan by his hair. And he had dropped Stan right into a cup of tea.

So the people called a town meeting. This time they picked the tallest man in Cedar Grove to challenge the giant. But Tall Tom was not a brave man. He did not want to meet the giant. But, at last, off he went.

Before the townspeople could count to
three, Tall Tom came running back.

"I just saw the giant break the tallest tree
in the forest in two pieces!" he cried. "I did
not want that to happen to me."

The people in the town did not know
what to do next.

"That does it! I am going to beat that giant," said Mickey. "I may be small. But I am not afraid.

"Before I go, I'll need three things. I'll need a bag. I'll need a drinking straw. And I'll need the whitest, roundest cheese in town. I have a plan!"

The people wondered what the
woodcutter wanted with such things. But they
gave him what he asked for. Then they told
him how to find the giant.

When the woodcutter got to the giant's cave, he looked everywhere. But he could not find the giant. So he walked into the deep, dark cave. There he found bats and rats. But there was no sign of the giant.

The woodcutter decided to wait for the giant. He hopped onto a rock outside the cave. Just then the rock began to shake.

"Wooooooooh! What is going on here?" cried Mickey.

"Ho, ho, ho!" came a rumbling noise from above.

The woodcutter looked up and up and up. "Oh, I see!" Mickey said. "You must be the giant!

"Well, I am very glad to meet you," said Mickey in a small voice.

"You mean you are not afraid of me?"
asked the giant.

"Afraid of you? Why, I am here to
challenge you," said Mickey.

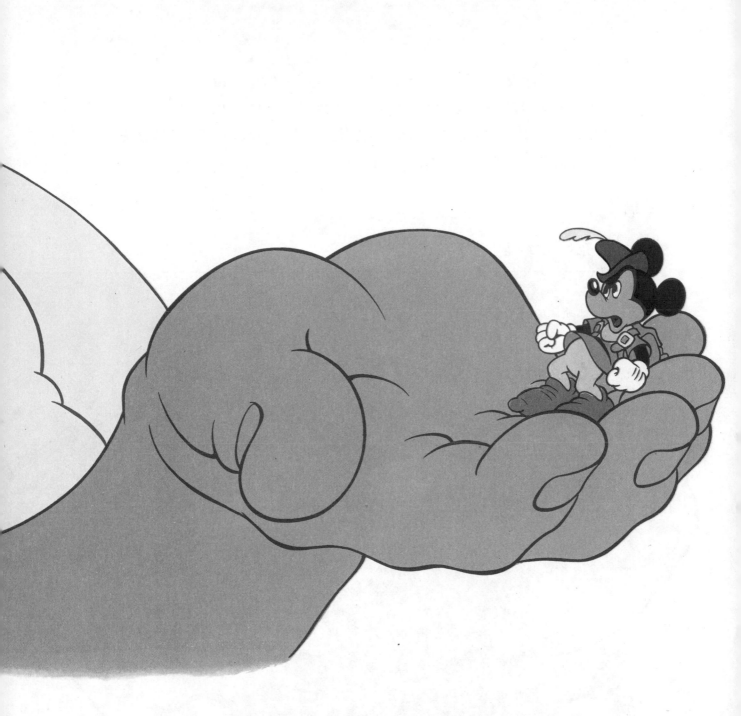

"Ho, ho, ho!" thundered the giant. "Bigger men than you have tried to beat me. They have failed. I'll just have to show you how strong I am!

"Watch this!" roared the giant. Then he wrapped his huge hand around the widest tree in the forest. He pulled it up as if it were a carrot from a garden.

"And this!" he said. Then he pounded his huge hand on the ground. The ground came apart. It became a deep, long canyon.

"Now it is my turn," said Mickey to the giant. "Watch how far I can blow this leaf."

"A leaf!" yelled the giant. "I could blow down fifty trees with one breath!" And the giant took a deep breath. *Whoooooooosh!* There lay fifty trees on the forest floor!

Mickey now knew his plan would work.
"Not bad," he told the giant. "Now it is
my turn. Watch how far I throw this stone."
"That is just a pebble!" said the giant.
"Step aside!" The giant bent down to pick up
a boulder.
"That is such a tiny rock!" cried Mickey.
"Why not throw the one over there?"

Mickey pointed to the very boulder that
was blocking the road to Cedar Grove.
    The giant gathered all his strength. He
threw that boulder far, far away. And now the
road was not blocked.

"My plan is working better than I had hoped," Mickey thought. He reached into his bag. He pulled out the straw. "Watch this," he said to the giant. "I am going to drink all the water in this pond."

"Straws and ponds are for weaklings,"
said the giant. "I can drink a lake!"
　　"Can you drink all those foot-shaped
lakes in the planting fields?" asked Mickey.
　　"Watch me," said the giant. And with
that, he drank all the water in each and every
lake!

Now the giant was tired. And he was so full of water that he was about to burst.

"Here is an easy one for you," said Mickey. "How much water can you squeeze from a stone?"

The giant picked up a stone. He squeezed it as hard as he could. But no water came from the stone.

"What kind of giant are you?" asked
Mickey. He held up the round, white cheese.
"See this stone? Watch this!" Then he
squeezed and squeezed. Water ran from
the cheese.

The giant's eyes grew big with fear.

"And if you don't leave Cedar Grove at
once," said Mickey, "why, I'll . . ."

The giant turned and ran.

Mickey smiled to himself. His plan had worked! He had stood up to the giant. And he had made the giant put right all of the wrong things he had done. Quickly he went back to town. He told the people what he had done.

They cheered Mickey for his courage. He
became the hero of the town. From that time
on, the people of Cedar Grove lived in peace.
And the giant was never heard from again.